Be Wee with Bea

-PART 3-

Learn To Begin Again

LIZ K. O'NEILL

CONTENTS

Acknowledgement .... *v*

About The Author .... *vii*

Dedication .... *ix*

A Note To The Reader .... *xi*

Introduction .... *xiii*

Preface .... *xv*

Chapter 1   No Benny Around 1

Chapter 2   What To Do With Zoe 5

Chapter 3   Willow Knows 9

Chapter 4   In The Meantime 13

Chapter 5   The Growly Puppy 17

Chapter 6   Many Plans Hatching 21

Chapter 7   A Conflicting Interruption 25

Chapter 8   Follow The Path 29

Chapter 9   The Rescue 33

Chapter 10   Zoe's Plan Is Played Out 37

Chapter 11   Maddie's Past 41

Chapter 12   Learning To Begin Again 45

Chapter 13   Down The Hill 49

Chapter 14   Stone By Stone....................................... 53

Chapter 15   A Cry For Help....................................... 57

Chapter 16   Snakely And Spidie Help 61

Chapter 17   The Get Away 65

Chapter 18   The Bird With The Guiding Light 69

Chapter 19   What Was vs What Can Be......................... 73

Chapter 20   Renewed 77

Chapter 21   Billie Bear 81

Chapter 22   Osala Bear... 85

Chapter 23   Wounded Moms................................... 89

Chapter 24   The Mystery Bag.................................. 93

Chapter 25   Foe Or Friend 97

Chapter 26   A Costume Contest............................... 101

Chapter 27   A Dear Joyous Wee Bear 105

Glossary 111

ACKNOWLEDGEMENT

I WOULD like to acknowledge in this 3rd book, my dear friend Sherrie French (stage name…Buddy bear) who has been there with me through it all. She has comforted me in the losses featured in the book, has listened to my thought process in my writing this series. I have featured her as a counselor for troubled animals because Sherrie is a psychiatric nurse.

Luck would have it for Annie and Sweet Puppy, there was a time when Sweet Puppy was visiting Doolie's with her mom, that she, who believed herself to be a hero puppy, found she was in the middle of a serious opportunity to fight for her crush, Annie, against Zoe. The power struggle became quite violent.

When Zoe and Annie were quarreling, Doolie made the same mistake Bea had during the Sweet Puppy and Scruffles fights. They didn't even seem to notice their mom was there trying to break them up. They were seeing nothing but red.

Doolie noticed Zoe, who was much larger and stronger than Annie had begun bullying her. This had gone on for long enough as far as Annie was concerned. She had had enough and began fighting back.

If anyone were to examine Annie, they'd realize Annie's nose was almost not there. She and Maddie both had flat faces, making it extremely difficult for them to bite anyone with much effectiveness. Although, Maddie did learn to nip at feet, Annie never could get the hang of it.

This clash was Sweet Puppy's opportunity to impress her crush Annie and to make a difference by protecting her as Benny would have if he weren't at the bridge of rainbows.

CHAPTER 2

What To Do With Zoe

SWEET PUPPY'S nose is like Zoe's; therefore, it is a fair fight. She is hoping Annie can see what a brave fighter she is. She began growling and biting at Zoe, hoping to scare her enough to get her to back-off. She has one eye on Zoe and the other on Annie.

Doolie was attempting to break up the vicious sparring match, or at least pull Annie to safety. Then it happened. Sweet Puppy was focused on the wrong movement and the next thing heard even over the growls was a pained-fill yowl.

As Doolie was reaching in to lift Annie out of the fiery fracas, Sweet Puppy chomped down hard with all of her might, believing it was Zoe going in for a frightful attack on Annie.

Sweet Puppy realized what she had done. She would never want to hurt Doolie. She felt just as terrible as she had when her mom got injured several times she and Scruffles were tangling.

Sweet Puppy regarded Doolie as her second mom. The cave room grew stressfully silent. Bea immediately coaxed a dazed Sweet Puppy over to her. The two trembled sitting on the cold cave floor, not from the cold but in fear of the consequences.

Bea's old fears returned. She was sure Doolie would tell both her and Sweet Puppy to leave immediately and never return. Doolie had that way about her. She was direct in her thoughts and emotions and it often frightened Bea.

However, Doolie also had a loving, understanding, caring part to her ability to solve problems. Bea fearing the worst, with 50 bees swirling around inside her, talked to the maker of dear best friends.

Those 50 bees, angrily buzzing within her, calmed. She heard the comforting sound of contented bees making honey, her "be good to myself" treat. She knew everything would balance out.

At first Doolie was angry at Sweet Puppy, but after a silence, and Bea thought maybe talking with the maker of moms who could become angry, Doolie became peaceful.

Bea heard Doolie reassure Sweet Puppy she knew she would never intentionally harm her second mom. It was then, Bea realized, she'd been holding her breath for a long time.

She let out a long bear sigh of relief.

Doolie and Sweet Puppy could not always be at Doolies which meant Zoe had the run of the cave halls. She would easily intimidate Annie, who made the mistake thinking she could take on Zoe.

This tragic misjudgment cost Annie her happiness and was her reason she knew she needed to head out for the bridge of rainbows. It also was the cause of Zoe having to go live with Bea and Sweet Puppy, never to return.

Both Zoe and Sweet Puppy loved playing together. Any fights they had, did not last long. That arrangement worked great until Doolie asked Bea to share her voluminous cave home. There were so many empty spaces with just Maddie still around, Doolie's empty heart was echoing loneliness.

Bea was torn thinking about the move. She spoke with Doolie about what to do with Zoe. Where could she possibly go? They both agreed that Zoe couldn't be living out in the wild with no one to care for her, but neither had an answer.

It looked as if Bea and Sweet Puppy would have to stay where they were, and Doolie and Maddie would just have to rattle around in their empty cave home. Bea and Doolie would never be able to spend time with each other again.

With the alternative arrangement, Sweet Puppy and Zoe would never play together again. There had to be a win-win situation. Doolie and Bea would not tolerate being separated from each other because of something that was not at all their fault.

It was Zoe's responsibility, she had badly hurt Annie. But they couldn't just tell her she had to fend for herself. As angry and hurt as Doolie may have been, fortunately for Zoe, Doolie was not one to hold a grudge and plan how to get even.

Doolie knew any meanness she showed toward Zoe, would not turn Annie around as she made her way on the path to the bridge of rainbows. There was no point in that thinking.

Bea hoped Doolie would talk to the maker about this situation or at least go to visit Willow, the one who was there through rain, storms of any kind and especially sunny days.

She knows when others have storms going on in their heads they especially need her to help them to see through the foggy, cloudy, dark things happening to them. If only Doolie would go see her.

CHAPTER 3

Willow Knows

DOOLIE REMEMBERED how much Willow helped her crew from what seemed long ago. Dear Benny and Zoe had cried to Willow how useless they felt because they had such intense anxiety.

They each told her how their fear caused them to behave in such a way that even though that reputation was the last thing they wanted; they couldn't help themselves.

She mentions the mission they had accepted, to free their mom, who after rescuing a horse being abused, was locked into a cage. The comforting tree tells the two self-doubting puppies that the rescue was only successful because of them.

They had actually tolerated Maddie, with her three legs to crawl across each of their backs, hike up their necks, reaching their heads to be able to stretch on her one little back leg to move the lever, to open the gate, to free their mom.

Willow emphasizes how even though both of them hated being touched and would snap at others in similar situations, during this very important, dangerous project, they did not object.

They both walked away from Willow feeling a little more sure of themselves and a little calmer. As Doolie recalled their meeting with Willow, she focused on what both Benny and Zoe had said about how their anxiety caused them to react to someone before they even realized it was happening.

Willow had believed them and didn't criticize them for not being able to instantly change their actions. This gave Doolie a reason to do the very same brain exercise as Bea does when she needs to prepare to do her talk to the maker.

Bea was also doing her talk to the maker to enable Doolie to come up with a solution to this terribly sad, awkward dilemma. There had to be a way. Willow might be able to unlock the answer to the problem just as Maddie who after crawling over grumpy Annie was able to do to free their mom.

There had to be a way to free Zoe, to save her, so she wasn't put out to be alone with no one to talk to or play with. She would probably be able to find food because she knew about the food on the edge of the dumpsters at the back of the buildings that is surrounded by that black stuff that covered all of the grasses and little trees.

Bea worried about how Zoe would be able to reach the food the humans left on the cover of the dumpsters. The confused puppy would need a bear mom to get to the top of the dumpster for her. She could never climb that high.

Bea began doing her scanning and planning exercise to try to think about how she could sneak out to help reach some food for Zoe. She remembered how she thought she would have to move into one of the dumpsters, to live, since she couldn't get herself back out of it.

She was panicking when she realized she was trapped until reliable Scruffles, her first guest, a raccoon cat, came to her rescue. So, who would come to the wee bear's rescue this time? Scruffles was at the bridge of rainbows and would not be able to suddenly appear to save his mom.

She felt guilty as she rethought rescuing Zoe for food. Her repetitive thinking returned. There must be, there has to be another way. She decided she'd just wait and not get stuck in her thoughts and worries.

She'd become stuck enough when she dropped her 'be good to myself' treat, honey. Her exercise of running in place made her legs very tired. When she got stuck like she was now, she couldn't do anything. Everything fun passed her by. All she could do was focus on what was keeping her stuck.

All of this anxiety evaporated when Bea got the message from Doolie that she decided to go to see Willow. It was because of Willow that Doolie finally thought of who could help Zoe and take her in.

CHAPTER 4

In The Meantime

IN THE meantime, Bea is doing some serious exercises which were part of her Be Wee With Bea exercise regime, established many cold cave nights ago. The number one choice is, of course, doing her stepstooling of going up and down a step stool to get clay pots of honey.

She smiles when she recalls some comical incidences that occurred whenever she dropped any of her "be good to myself" treat while doing her fine motor weight lifting. She was sometimes too enthusiastic about using her paw to lift gobs of honey from the pot to the mouth.

Not wanting to waste a drop of honey, this necessitated a new exercise called toe touching, which required her to bend over to earnestly clean her gooey toes. If she saw need to bend over further to the floor, she was entering into the next phase known as floor touching.

However, these were not the exercises Bea felt an urge to practice. Doing her notice exercise, she recognized her plotting to figure out how to solve Zoe's problem may actually work out.

Her usual exercise of scanning and planning was changing before her very eyes. Only once had she seen when help from her was actually requested. Usually, the outcome of a dilemma was basically none of her business.

This time, she was involving the maker of wayward misunderstood puppies in this project. Her brain exercise where she did serious thinking and meditation to calm her thoughts enabled her to do her talk to the maker.

Her next move was to locate Doolie to see how far she and Willow had gotten in finding a solution. Bea the genius wee bear had a solution and she knew it could work.

Her strolling picked up speed, thus she arrived at her desired destination in no time, a bit out of breath, but she was there. Doolie and Willow were in deep conversation. She hesitated to do her usual barging into a couple or even a group involved in discussion.

She stood silently awaiting the signal to proceed. What she overheard fit perfectly with her imagined plan. It was going to work out so there was a place for Zoe to live and neither she nor Sweet Puppy would have to be sad.

In the meantime, as Doolie and Willow spoke, Doolie remembered both she and Bea had a friend who Zoe always trusted more than anyone else. Everyone's friend, Buddy bear had spent time helping troubled animals who had great anxiety as a result of the way their owners had treated them.

Because a lot of the problems centered around food, with the vast experience Buddy bear had, she was the right one to have Zoe move in with.

Buddy bear worked with new ideas for the best ways to feed stressed animals, who just didn't seem to be able to find any appetite. Every time they were presented with food, all they could think of was a human yelling at them, throwing food at them, or ignoring them.

That was Bea's cue to add her ideas. She told them that Zoe could spend her time with Bea and Sweet Puppy. When the two went to spend time with Doolie and her family, Zoe could stay with Stormy and Buddy bear.

Of course, this all had to be cleared with Buddy bear and Stormy, but everyone liked the idea. It was so relieving for Doolie, who loved Zoe, but didn't like her for what she did to Annie.

There was more discussion about precautions that needed to be taken. It seemed that Zoe reacted violently when she felt what we call insecure and jealous. Bea's metaphor was that Zoe was like an older puppy who feels insignificant when a new puppy is born.

That older puppy watches the mom and sees only how the mom spends, of necessity, more time with the new pup. She does not see that the mom is so thankful that her big puppy can do so much for herself that it makes things easier for her mom.

When Zoe was around other puppies like Annie, she believed that Doolie loved Annie more than her. She might also be just aggressive with any other puppies so both Bea and Buddy bear would have to figure out a preventative exercise. Bea remembered the exercise she'd learned that alerted her to be on guard but calm.

When presented with the idea, Buddy bear discussed it with her puppy Stormy, who had lived with her for many cold snows. Stormy didn't seem to have a fighting bone in his body. They talked about how bad a life Zoe had had before Doolie discovered her.

Zoe had told Doolie that the people she'd lived with did not understand that she was not, nor could ever be the dog they'd had before her. It seemed they were unable to let her be herself. That's all she'd wanted, for them to see who she was, not who they wanted her to be.

CHAPTER 5

The Growly Puppy

STORMY WAS very moved by Zoe's backstory and agreed he believed both he and his mom could make a difference in Zoe's life. He thought it was a great idea.

When Buddy bear cautioned Stormy that Zoe might want to start a fight with him, he said he understood how that worked. Such behavior was familiar to him. In the group of puppies, he'd lived with before she found him, there was one puppy who was very angry causing fear among the other animals, so they'd do what he wanted.

He grew serious as he continued to report to his mom that the intimidated, weaker puppies did just what the bullying puppy wanted. He confidently told how he called the mean, growly puppy's bluff and just ignored him.

It is set, then, Zoe will live with Bea and Sweet Puppy, however when they went to spend time with Doolie, she will stay with Buddy bear and Stormy. This worked out well with Stormy and Buddy bear's vigilance.

At first Zoe was practicing her best manners, but when she thought Buddy bear was too busy to notice, she began to do just as Stormy had predicted. She exhibited the same intimidating behaviors which Stormy was acquainted with, from experience.

When Stormy was trying to get past Zoe to reach the opening of their cave home, Zoe began circling him, showing her teeth, growling, and plunking herself in front of him to block his way.

To Zoe's surprise, that wise and prepared puppy, Stormy, just went around her. He kept his promise, of how he'd respond if Zoe came to live with them and began acting out. He believed she didn't really want to fight, she just wanted to be accepted and loved. The insightful puppy knew she was very anxious and confused and decided he'd tell her that someday.

In the meantime, while Stormy had made things so much easier for Buddy bear, times were not always as smooth among the wee Bea home cave walls. This was a whole other mix or what we might call a whole other kettle of fish.

Call it what we want, it did not bode well for Bea. There was a lovely, peaceful routine with the two puppies playing tirelessly. This assured Bea, she could leave them unattended while she went for her daily stroll.

She knows no one will consider her a bad mom, if she leaves them alone for a while. They are certainly old enough to be left alone. You see, Bea was aware the problems did not arise while she was gone, but when she got back from being away.

This gave her all the more reason to have some time to herself. She was, as her mom would call it, practicing a "be good to myself" exercise, in a different way. This did not involve her "be good to myself "treat. This called for fresh air as she did her notice exercise.

She felt young again, strolling, listening to the wind cry as the cool air licked her face. She heard new sounds of birds chattering about something important to them. This carried her desire in doing her talk to the maker. The next plan that arose was to visit her dear tree friend, Willow.

Strolling in that direction, Bea was reminded of the day she discovered Willow weeping. The cause was not that she'd been hurt by the children who came to vent to her, but her reason was she felt she never did enough for them.

She also said she was weeping because she felt the deep pain of the children, who were extremely wounded in every way. She did mention, children told her about happenings they never told anyone else.

These little ones, hiding aching, broken, hearts, believed she would hold their stories in the core of her being. Bea was certain, they were right to trust her. She would tell no one and was very careful how much she told Bea.

Bea always wished there was something she could do for Willow. She'd done so much for Bea and all of her friends. The list in her memory was long, with several having already gone to the bridge of rainbows. There was Benny, Scruffles, and now Annie.

That caring tree helped save a very good friendship among, Scruffles, Sweet Puppy and her. At first, it didn't look like things were going to work out for Sweet Puppy. Previous to Sweet Puppy's arrival, Bea, the mom, had set up a convenient routine between her and Scruffles.

Somehow there could be found a big heart in a wee bear. Her trusting relationship with the maker, caused that wee heart to grow increasingly, until there was actually room in it for a ragged raccoon cat.

CHAPTER 6

Many Plans Hatching

SHE CAN'T resist bringing Sweet Puppy home. That's what Bea names her because she had introduced herself as carrying the name Bea also. There can never be two Beas, that would be too confusing. Sometimes, rarely, but once in a while, our wee bear did things simply. This was one of them.

When she first met Scruffles, he introduced himself as Scruffy. He certainly was, along with his terrible story which merited such a name. Bea was not opposed to changing any original given names.

As Scruffy began to eat well and bathe in the fishing river, he looked increasingly better and less and less like his name. That is when Bea changed his name to Scruffles.

The dignity this gave him might carry our imagination to a cat adorned with a prim and proper bowtie. You choose the color and pattern. In case you do not know who, I am, I am the narrator who was long ago, introduced to Bea by Timothy. He was her furniture carving, clay pot making beaver who had a lodge in a body of water Bea named Timothy's Pond.

Now, on with our story, which is becoming a cautionary tale for all. Because of Sweet Puppy's unacceptable treatment of her host, Scruffles, Bea was seriously considering changing Sweet Puppy's name to Not So Sweet Puppy.

This is how Willow intervened at just the right time. She encouraged Bea to put her foot, paws and claws down. Bea was to review the cave rules for Sweet Puppy. Bea, herself, was not to get physically entwined anymore. It was too dangerous.

Bea did as advised and it worked out splendidly. Now she was confronted with a similar ugly situation. Hopefully, Willow could help. When Bea began relating her saga, she recognized herself to be more upset than she'd originally thought.

After Willow persuaded her to slow her phrases down a bit, she was able to get the picture Bea was describing. It seemed things went smoothly if Bea was already in the section of the cave, she practiced her Be Wee With Bea exercises.

Even as she did her stepstooling exercise, the two little ones played, forgetting all about their mom. It was when she came home and the two met her at the same time, she couldn't greet either one, for fear of a competitive scuffle.

Zoe seemed to forget that Bea knew Sweet Puppy better, they'd been together much longer. Zoe had been with Doolie. She wanted Bea, her new mom all to herself. This was something that a confused Sweet Puppy did not understand and was wearying of.

And yet, possibly Sweet Puppy did know exactly what was going on with Zoe. It wasn't that long ago, Sweet Puppy could have forgotten how she behaved around Scruffles, taunting him as she did. So now, the situation was reversed.

Being filled in with the background was a great help to Willow, but so far, had done nothing for Bea. What was she ever to do? Willow had the answer to that question.

Willow suggested Bea practice her investigation exercise before entering. As she did her alert but calm exercise, she stopped at the opening of the cave home, as Willow had directed her to do. She needed to see and hear where the two puppies were.

When she realized they were in a back room talking, she slipped in and when they saw her, she was doing her stepstooling exercise. It was clearly time for her "be good to myself" treat.

She was so nervous with shaking paws; she spilled a little on her toes. That was actually more fun for her as she did her toe touching exercise. Being as preoccupied as she was, she did not notice the two puppies laughing as she stood back up.

It was as if they didn't notice she'd just returned. Willow was so wise to have thought of this non-troublesome approach. She thought it would even work if they weren't in a back room. She'd just wait until the way was clear.

The opportunity arises for Bea's plan to be tested. Sweet Puppy and her mom are going to stay at Doolie's for an extended period of time. This means Zoe will be spending a greater number of days with Buddy bear and Stormy.

As Zoe became more comfortable with her new cave home, she began strutting around Stormy, who as promised, ignored her. When Buddy bear and Stormy went for strolls, it was as if Zoe were memorizing her surroundings. She doesn't say much, however, seems to be doing a lot of looking, studying and planning.

CHAPTER 7

A Conflicting Interruption

BUDDY BEAR isn't sure what is going on in Zoe's busy head, but suspects it is not safe. Although, Zoe may have seen it as safe for her, possibly a way out. Neither of them discussed anything about it. Buddy bear just watched Zoe more closely as plans were hatched.

When she stayed with them, Zoe seemed to be adjusting and conforming, leaving Stormy alone. Buddy bear found things Zoe liked to eat and knew how to talk with her. That clever mom bear actually got her to talk about why she didn't eat.

Zoe became aware of a fact she could not deny. Refusing to eat was a way of keeping herself safe with no one able to tell her what to do. When Buddy bear heard this, it was similar to what was claimed by the other non-eating animals she had helped in the past.

She explained to Zoe as she had others, that it was only in her imagination that she was stopping anyone from telling her what to do. Buddy bear wanted Zoe to realize this attitude and behavior made her more unhappy.

She was fairly certain what Zoe would say if she asked about hunger. As others had told her, Zoe said the empty feeling in her stomach kept her from thinking about how unhappy she was and how little she liked herself.

Both Stormy and Buddy bear reassured her that if she hung around them, she'd begin to feel better about herself and would want to eat. Zoe, said she'd try. Buddy bear knew the same as Willow that trying leaves two choices.

When someone tries, they either succeed or fail, there's no in-between. If we work at something, it's little by little. We gradually arrive and can feel successful. By Zoe saying she'd try, it meant nothing.

Buddy bear knew that most times when the animals she worked with said that they would try, they probably weren't going to do anything. She was still quite concerned what was going to happen with that situation.

Her suspicions grow when she does her notice exercise while they are on their walks. Stormy even mentions he had a weird feeling about the way Zoe acted when they were in a specific area of the woods.

Tensions heightened for Buddy bear and Stormy. What they had discussed and practiced was going to soon become real. Bea and Sweet Puppy were moving in with Doolie and Maddie.

They'd been going to Doolie's so much, she asked Bea if she and Sweet Puppy were ready to move in with her and Maddie. Bea was thrilled. Annie was thrilled. Her crush on Sweet Puppy had only grown stronger.

Maddie was growing on Sweet Puppy. Since there was no Annie to distract her, Sweet Puppy noticed Maddie. She realized what a funny personality and courage she had. It stopped Sweet Puppy from feeling sorry for herself every time. She just had to look over at Maddie's three legs and then look down at her own four legs and be thankful.

Bea's packing for Sweet Puppy and her new home with Maddie and Doolie was interrupted by a mysterious disruption outside her cave. The howling and yelping of some wounded animal sounded very near.

Curious and concerned, doing her investigation exercise, Bea looked toward the opening of her cave home. She needed to discover what the cause of the cacophonous commotion was. When she stepped outside, her wee bear eyes grew large with disbelief and concern.

Bea wondered why this little, fragile one would have come all this way? What could have happened. She was crying and shaking so severely that Bea could not understand a word she was saying.

The dear creature had tipped over onto the hard packed dirt, but didn't seem to notice the stones digging into her thin fur and skin. Something dreadful had numbed her to anything in her surroundings.

Bea didn't quite know what to do. She tried getting the sobbing puppy's attention. She remembered how as a young pup, she and her mom were in a wide field during a vicious thunder and lightning storm. She was so frantic; her mom could only get her attention by kindly looking her right in her eyes.

Doing her notice exercise, Bea observes the same terror in the sobbing and curling up posture she had demonstrated long ago on that fated day. Her attention sharpened with her eyes fixed toward the longing, tear filled face in front of her.

Remembering how difficult it was to see her mother through her clouded tears, Bea isn't even sure if she could be seen now. This wee bear, was hesitant to disturb Sweet Puppy, who had been ailing with pain lately.

She'd never be able to make the long-required trek. The caring, conflicted mom didn't feel right leaving Sweet Puppy alone. This was no time for her puppy to feel abandoned. She was the mom who was supposed to protect her little one.

The greatly conflicted wee bear glances in the direction of a weakened, resting Sweet Puppy, then at the defenseless creature rolling around on the packed dirt in front of her.

CHAPTER 8

Follow The Path

BEA IS conflicted and yet, she needs to follow the path laid out for her. The maker is asking something of the wee brave bear. She had the same fifty bees darting in every direction inside her as she had, many leaf-filled trees ago.

When she just knew something was very wrong with her favorite path that she named Bea's Golden Path. The maker always seemed to give her clues when something was wrong around her. There was that same sinking feeling she'd had when she was sure a buzzing and crashing sound meant danger for Willow.

Trees were being sawed down. Fortunately, Willow was safe. Bea noticed the 50 bees did not cease their deafening humming, meaning definite trouble. This time things would not be all right. Even doing her talk to the maker didn't help.

She stared at the pathetic picture of the puppy slowly calming enough to be able to speak clearly and be understood. Bea thought she must have been exhausted running on her three little legs all that distance.

Bending down, Bea found the courage to ask Maddie what had happened that she'd hippety-skipped all this way from her home, soon to be filled with Sweet Puppy and her.

A shattered Maddie still only mumbles the message through a very wet, flat-nosed face. Bea is able to pick out a few words such as 'fell' and 'head' which gives her no real clue to solving the shaky situation.

Bea understood Maddie to yell that it was too late anyway and that somebody'd already gone. The wee flabbergasted bear needed to get to the bottom of that garbled message and fill in the missing words.

When calmly asked, the hysterical puppy was able to answer the question about what happened when she whimpered that someone fell. Bea felt she was making progress and decided to ask if Maddie could tell her who fell.

Bea turned pale under her fur, and her mouth fell open as she heard Maddie say that Doolie had fallen. It was when Bea asked if there was anything she could do, that the rest of the tragic tale was completed.

Maddie finished the whole topic off by telling Bea that Doolie had already left for the bridge of rainbows, but that she left the message that Bea and Sweet Puppy should still move in and join Maddie. That way Maddie will not have to relocate to Bea's cave home.

Bea has a difficult time believing that Doolie is really gone, that the next time she and Sweet Puppy enter Doolie's cave home, only Maddie will be there.

She invited Maddie in to rest and to have a drink of water, which was important after being upset and hippity-skipping such a great distance on three exceptionally short legs.

As the devastated bear continued to walk, she stumbled over the bump at the entrance of the cave. Her vision became distorted as thick tears filled her eyes. She wanted so much to do her pretend exercise, but nothing worked.

She didn't even care that her whimpering could be heard as she went to Sweet Puppy to give her the tragic news. A river of tears could have formed on the cave floor if the degree of sadness could be measured.

Bea felt an urgency to finish packing to plan the journey to their new home. She considered possibly inviting Buddy bear, Stormy, and Zoe to visit. She wasn't sure how it would affect Zoe.

The considerate wee bear didn't want to start any trouble for Buddy bear. They hadn't talked much about how Zoe and Stormy were adjusting to each other and how Zoe was situating herself in Buddy bear's cave home.

Sometimes Bea wished for her mom, or for the early days when Scruffles and her were alone, even before Sweet Puppy. Things were simpler then. No one was making any trips to the bridge of rainbows. It was a happier time.

Some might wonder why Bea is not mentioning her dear friend Timothy the Beaver, who carved all her furniture, her step-stooler and the cupboard with shelves she has filled with her "be good to myself' treat.

The golden honey which sustains her in all situations, joyful and sad is stored in the clay pots he fashioned from the clay soil around his pond known as Timothy's Pond.

Timothy was not at the bridge of rainbows, however, unfortunately he was also not at Timothy's Pond. As Bea was having to do, Timothy had moved on, to begin again.

Beavers mate for life, nevertheless, his first mate had left him because he didn't work hard enough and fast enough at rebuilding the dam to their pond. Timothy had told Bea how it made his beaver mind swirl when his mate wanted him to build a dam in a spot that would never do. He knew it would keep breaking because it was right in the swiftest currents of their river.

Timothy had a feeling of emptiness and loss since she left. He mentioned how important Bea was to him. Even though she was not a beaver, she was his best friend.

CHAPTER 9

The Rescue

BEA ALWAYS thought the concept of 'best friend' was confounding. She wondered if someone said she was their best friend, did that mean they had to be her best friend? Even though the word 'best' gives you the idea there is only one.

Bea had many best friends, who had all gone to the bridge of rainbows. Did that mean she had no special friends. But Willow was definitely on that list in her head and heart. She hoped Willow felt the same about her. She thought she might ask her that someday.

She remembered what her mom had told her about potential friends. They can be anywhere, just to be on guard and do your notice exercise. She guessed that Timothy must have dared to trust the new friend he had met.

They must have become very close friends; she must have been persuasive. He left with her. There was no more need for any signaling slaps on the water. Bea knew, if she slapped the prescribed two loud slaps, there would be no one loud beaver tail slap in response. He was gone.

She almost wanted to slap the two signaling slaps to see if, possibly, Timothy hadn't left and was still in the lodge, his protective home. He was in another lodge, finally happier with his life. He would no longer feel like an empty clay pot.

Bea reminded Willow that she had told the sad wee bear that she would feel better about everything if she talked about all of her friends who were no longer with her.

It struck her there was no place to visit anymore. Doolie and her crew were all gone to the bridge of rainbows, and Timothy was nowhere to be found.

Her wandering, drooping mind was quickly grounded with a visit from Buddy bear. Her cave home was in the deep woods quite far from Bea's cave. It seemed like a perfect place for Zoe to live. If she set her mind on an idea, there it stayed.

If she planned to run away from there, we humans would advise that she pack a big lunch and bring a map. Bea did not look forward to the long-rugged stroll. But when she heard Buddy bear or Stormy's story, she knew they'd better hurry.

Stormy had run to his mom Buddy bear to tell her that Zoe had run down the hill without saying anything. When Stormy yelled for her to stop, she just continued running, as if she hadn't heard him.

Buddy bear knew very well that Zoe had heard Stormy. Stormy was beginning to cry for several reasons. He was angry, concerned, and he felt responsible. He felt he should have been able to do something.

His mom reminded him that they had talked about how this might happen. They were suspicious of Zoe's actions every time they went for a walk. They didn't know of what plan to make, just go look for her.

Bea notified Sweet Puppy of Zoe's new antics, so she readied herself. They informed Maddie that they'd be back before dark. Maddie assured them that she'd be fine. Sweet Puppy agreed to stay back to be with Maddie.

Maddie urged Sweet Puppy to go along with her mom. The more looking for Zoe, the better. She felt a little helpless, until she remembered Willow's words the time, she met with her.

Some very powerful things happened when their mom, who was now at the bridge of rainbows took them to talk with Willow. That wonderful listening tree helped Maddie and all of the family realize how important they were.

Their mom was locked in a large securely wired crate and the brave puppies had to rescue her. The backstory is, when Doolie was younger, she had to be rescued by a horse. She had fallen into a deep hole used for a trap.

The grateful wise bear promised the kind horse that when she got a chance, she would pay him back by helping another horse in need of attention. That moment presented itself, bringing us up to her second occasion needing to be rescued. This time it was by her own family of puppies

A man was being mean to a horse who was locked in behind a fence. Doolie hid until the man left and went into his house. She slowly, step by step made it over to the gate and lifted the wood that locked him in.

She was not fast enough. The man must have only needed to go into his house to get something. Since the horse is away free, the man rage, and Doolie the rescuer is going to pay for it.

He has his shotgun or as Doolie and her mom called it a black stick that shot out things worse than pebbles. Remembering this, Doolie does not try to fight him off. She is rushed into a large wire crate, locked in and just left there.

CHAPTER 10

Zoe's Plan Is Played Out

WE CONTINUE with Maddie's celebratory memory. Doolie, the captive bear needs her puppies to come by soon to help her escape. Tussling and playing around, delays them from being very close behind her. She prepares herself, practicing in her mind how she will get their attention.

Growing anxious, she just wished they'd hurry. She didn't want that human to come back out to where she was, especially carrying a black stick. The shaking caged bear had no idea what his plan for her was, but was sure it wasn't good.

Because they had no idea what it meant to be quiet, Doolie knew she would be alerted to their nearing the area. Her crew did not disappoint, she could hear them coming down the path. What she had practiced repeatedly in her imagination would definitely get their attention.

Doolie let loose a growl, shaking the cage and the ground they all stood upon. Leaves even began to fall as the branches shook. She had their attention and motioned them over to her cage.

The plan was for Maddie to climb across a usually grumpy, Annie, onto a nervous Zoe and all the way up the long high neck of Benny. She needed to avoid his snapping jaws, on her way to the tippy-top of his head. On her one super strong back leg, she was to reach up as tall as she could to unlatch the door to her mom, Doolie's cage.

Amazingly, Annie did not grump once, Zoe stood as still as she could, Benny was able to keep his jaws clamped, and Maddie's little leg remained sturdy without any shaking.

The lever to the door was raised. Their mom was free and whisked them away from danger. This is what Willow had reminded and praised them each about. Maddie had never forgotten it. She could be brave even if Sweet Puppy left to help look for Zoe who had run away from Buddy bear's.

Believing Maddie was being honest about feeling confident to be alone, Sweet Puppy asked one more time and was shooed away by Maddie with mutual laughs.

She, her mom and Buddy bear made good time getting to Buddy bear's place. Stormy had remained behind in case Zoe returned. A disappointed Stormy had to report there was still no sign of their runaway friend.

Down the hill they trekked. Both Buddy bear and Stormy filled in Sweet Puppy and Bea as to some of their clues they had drawn observing Zoe every time they went for a walk in that area. There was a spot she always stopped at with a dreamy look in her eyes.

Buddy bear explained those were the times she knew Zoe was up to something. It seemed no matter how on guard and alert they were, strategic, deceptive Zoe outwitted them. With her thinking she was so clever, there was concern she might be in danger.

They split up to be able to cover the extensive terrain more quickly. Bea had a sense Zoe was somewhere by the river, but noticed Stormy was headed that way. She wanted to let Stormy be the hero to have located Zoe.

It wasn't long before Stormy came running to tell everyone he'd found Zoe. The complication was Zoe was trapped and couldn't move. Stormy reported Zoe was shivering, crying and having trouble breathing.

When Buddy bear reached Zoe's spot, she observed Zoe's state of difficulty and her traumatic condition. Her hindquarters were hanging off a bank being pummeled by the punishing current and her legs had sunk into the mud, holding her fast, unable to move at all.

Everyone dug around her 'til she was loosened and could get up on her own. Her legs were shaky under her, but she was able to move toward home. Buddy bear pointed out to her how many came to help.

It was impressed upon her as a message for her to know how many cares about her and how worried everyone was. Zoe shook her head at it all. She told Buddy bear she figured she would definitely be put out of the family after such a performance.

Zoe sobbed when Buddy bear motioned to her to come get a big bear hug. She reassured Zoe she was a member of their family and that wasn't going to change, even though it looked like Zoe had tested that out.

It was time for Bea and Sweet Puppy to get back to Maddie, who had already been alone too long. She figured Buddy bear, Stormy and Zoe would work things out and hopefully, there would be no repeat of this.

Maddie's little bobtail vibrated back forth, up and down she was so happy to see her new mom, Bea, and of course her longtime crush Sweet Puppy who took time to tell her everything she had missed. Maddie was in her glory having Sweet Puppy paying her so much attention.

CHAPTER 11

Maddie's Past

MADDIE HAD an extremely difficult beginning in a building full of cages where heartless humans made her care for baby pups without a rest. She told how one of the caring humans must have reported the abusive setting to someone.

They soon came to put a stop to the cruelty. The little momma puppies were set free and no longer kept prisoner. When she met Doolie her life changed for the better. She had discovered a wonderful, loving family, where she knew she belonged.

Because life had been so hard for her, she claimed her body was worn out. Increasingly losing her strength, resting more often was required. Sweet Puppy remarked to her mom how she noticed Maddie was sleeping more and more.

Bea fears Maddie is going to need assistance to get to the path of goodbyes. A few days later, Maddie announces she knows it is time for her to head out on the path to the bridge of rainbows.

She looked forward to seeing her crush, Bennie, and her mom, who she missed so much. Both Sweet Puppy and Bea with tears in their eyes offered to walk with her 'til it was time for her to leave them behind.

They both remembered what occurred when they walked with Scruffles. One minute he was strolling beside them, they turned away, then back. He was no more.

Maddie agreed to let them come along. The same thing happened. They could not have predicted, that when they looked away one particular time, and turned back to talk to her, she'd be gone.

Bea and Sweet Puppy continued to live in the cave Doolie originally set up. Sometimes it felt like the memories of laughter and fun were dancing along the walls. At those moments, she wished to be able to forget the before.

Next, it was Sweet Puppy's turn to head for the bridge of rainbows. She was having more difficulty walking as time went on. She, with tear-filled eyes, told Bea it was urgent she left before she could no longer walk.

Bea assured her of assistance getting to the beginning of the path and she'd walk her as far along the path as necessary.

With no one to share space with her in the large cave with her, Bea felt like a single leaf she's seen spinning around on the branch, resisting letting go.

She resolved there would to be another heartbeat echoing off the walls, in addition to spidies and a field mouse or two. She needed a new idea for this situation.

Doing her talk to the maker helped her remember to do her brain exercise. She did not feel as wretched. The one who would have fresh ideas was Willow, who told her to be like the water she heard singing.

She reminded the lost wee bear she herself stated of how much she'd learned from noticing the flow of the water. Bea wanted to practice being like the water as it slid around and over the rocks that would otherwise block it.

The stream will not let itself get stuck. Even in Timothy's dam, the water seeped through, over or under the logs. The current moved on to new surroundings for new adventures.

Willow helped the lonely wee bear figure out what she could do to get beyond moments of loneliness.

Requesting Bea do her problem-solving exercise and picture what she would do if the honey pots were empty. She knew she would go ask a friend or go looking for a honey tree.

Friends were like honey. That caring tree who spoke only the truth told Bea it was time she explored new paths to see what surprises, adventures and friends would reveal themselves.

It is up to Bea to find new friends. Willow was aware it was a great risk for the cautious bear, but she needed to get out strolling again. Bea had forgotten how to enjoy strolling. Sweet Puppy, who was last to go down the path to the bridge of rainbows, had made strolling fun.

Bea had difficulty following orders as a child, and not much had changed. She found herself, contrary to Willow's advice, journeying on the worn memory paths that had brought the most frustration and sense of not doing so well.

She revisits the location where, as she, Scruffles, and Sweet Puppy were doing an investigation exercise. This brought them to a terrible stuck-up surprise when they ended up in a group of mature burdock bushes. The green ones would not have been as messy.

She laughs as she remembers how she, Scruffles, and Sweet Puppy had shamefacedly limped home to rush to the fishing river to wash those light brown sticking balls off their faces, ears, arms, legs and tails.

CHAPTER 12

Learning To Begin Again

BEA'S MOST favorite accomplishment was discovering the signal stones left by the stone pilers who were older than the caves. We call these stone pilers Native Americans or Indigenous. Those structures gave her an idea of how to use a signal for the three of them to turn in a safe direction.

On one of their missions, while it was still dark, they had gone the wrong way and ended up falling down a loose dirt bank into the river. This idea of stone piling would show them the correct direction to travel before the large warm ball of brightness rose, so they could be safe.

Bea is very aware of her job to keep the young ones free from harm. She blames herself for not thinking of this before. But that was then. Sometimes she wishes with all of her wee bear heart she could forget the then part of her life.

Now she will stop for a short time at Bea's Golden Path to do her notice exercise. She has to do her talk to the maker about the black stuff smothering her favorite place to stroll, where, she used to dance around leaving pictures of her claws, paws and feet.

On another occasion, she'd joyfully observed, the black stuff slightly cracked, and plants and trees peeking out. This time, life more than peeks out. The brave trees, flowers and bushes are stretching as tall as they are able.

These give her an idea to share with Willow. She longed to practice the courage of the bright flowers, the color of the ball in the sky. They seemed to be able to find their way back through the darkness after every cold, icy time. This determined bear wanted to learn how to dig her way out of the darkness she'd been in.

Bea revealed to Willow she always wondered if the flowers she hoped to see again would be able to return. She happily reported, as it became warmer and brighter, they greeted her with joy.

The pensive bear wondered if they were carrying a message thing would get lighter and better in her life. Bea admitted to Willow, she believed the story those flowers told.

Willow reminded Bea, no one could avoid loss and pain or dark moments. But the maker, and our friends, new or old, would help each other get through the hard times to find answers.

The insightful tree explained, sometimes those searching for answers would need to carry the questions with them to finally put them down to pick up the answers.

Willow told Bea she did not want to see her dear bear friend become discouraged. She reviewed with Bea the image she had described of herself crawling, with feet, paws and claws, out of the dark empty cave. Bea began to realize she was the only one who could make that possible for herself.

Bea believed the maker would lead her to the right path, where new friends and answers could be discovered. She backtracked to her cave home, with the focus on her stepstooling exercise. Careful not to drop any, she lifted down the clay jars filled with her "be good to myself" treat.

Practicing that important exercise restored her courage to do her strolling alone. She admitted to herself she had done her exercise alone before. In fact, most of the time she'd been alone.

This felt like a different kind of 'alone', though. As she walked into the light, she noticed she had a friend walking beside her. She was not really alone after all. Her newly discovered friend danced, twirled, and played hide and seek. When Bea wasn't looking, her friend hid behind the trees.

She wondered why, when she asked question after question, there was no response. She noticed there was silence the entire time, which made the curious bear wonder if her sad friend felt lonely too. Bea does not realize she has her shadow following her.

Bea continued to follow an entirely new path leading her across a wooden bridge with singing water beneath it. She felt the maker of fishing rivers wanted her to cross the bridge, to go down to the water, to listen to the stones and pebbles tinkling against each other.

The hesitant wee bear looked at how fast the streams of water between the rocks were passing under the bridge. She did her notice exercise watching the leaves on one side of the bridge which, in the little time it took to walk to the other side of the bridge, were little dots going away from her.

Bea worries, if without taking extreme caution, she might be like the leaves carried along by the swift stream. She does not understand why the maker of wee bears would ask her to take such a great, dangerous risk.

CHAPTER 13

Down The Hill

JUST THINKING about trying to get down the rocky embankment made her fears grow. Then she remembered what Willow said about trying. Bea laughed a little to think Willow had used climbing up a bank as an example about trying. Ironically, she was climbing down a hill.

Bea wondered if what Willow had said in her talk about going up a hill would work for going down. Her traumatic situation of the time she shinnied up a tall tree to get Timothy some delicious, tender twigs flashed back. Going up was okay as long as she did not look down, but going back down was terrifying.

In telling Willow about it, Bea was helped to realize she was able to safely descend the tree because it was accomplished step by step. If she changed her approach about trying to do something, she would succeed.

She had pointed out to Bea the only results from trying are succeed or fail. But working at something step-by-step guarantees success every time. When Bea asked the wise tree her usual "what if's," she was reminded it was one of her favorite series of questions.

Bea laughed because she had to admit Willow knew her too well. She paused and asked her question about this hill Willow was discussing. She worried what if she slid back down part of it, while working to make it up to the top.

It was Willow's turn to ask the questions. She really got Bea to do her brain exercise when she asked her what would she have learned just before slipping back down the hill she was climbing.

After looking upward and tapping her paw to her head she knew the answer was she'd know where not to put her paws, claws and feet. Willow praised her for learning so quickly, the next time she would know to put her feet, paws and claws in a different spot.

She encouraged the wee learner that was the way she would make it up the hill, even if she repeatedly slid back down. Eventually arriving there would bring on a glorious feeling of success.

Bea decided way back then to practice a new exercise she would call "little by little." As she glanced down over the bridge she had been standing on, she knew it was time to practice her little-by-little exercise.

The fifty bees began buzzing inside her as her fears grew even greater. Talking to the maker of steep banks, she still did not know why the maker wanted her to go down that scary bank.

Something strange happened she just did not understand. The fifty bees were replaced by sweet humming bees. These were kind that made her "be good to myself" treat. She sure could use some of that golden sweetness right then.

But she knew the shelves and shelves of honey-filled clay pots were back in her cave home, a place she greatly longed for. She was farther away from home than she'd ever been alone, in severely unknown territory. Even her newfound friend had disappeared. She only danced around her when the golden globe in the sky was smiling on her.

The gentle humming usually meant things would be okay, however, she could see no possibility of that. As she hesitantly shuffled closer to the edge, she did her investigation exercise and doing her notice exercise, she saw it had a nice level dirt path she could quite easily walk down step by step, little by little.

As usual, all the fuss was for nothing, but she still saw no reason for the maker to lead her in this direction, down a steep path. Doing her notice exercise, she saw it before reaching the yellowed grass at the bottom of the path and had no idea what it meant or who made it.

She was so mesmerized by the strange sight she couldn't even do her brain exercise enough to be able to begin her investigation exercise. A sizzing sound startled her as she stood there staring across the river.

She heard a tiny voice say something like, didn't she think it was a nice likeness. First of all, she couldn't see anyone, besides she believed herself to be alone with this magnificent mystery.

She checked for her friend, wondering if she had said it. Her friend slowly appeared as the golden globe gave more light for Bea to see her. She asked her hide and seek companion if she had said anything?

There was silence as expected, but the voice asked her why she was talking to herself. The voice claimed, it was the one that spoke to her. Getting nowhere with this puzzle, Bea tipped her head back and looked up toward the bridge, her last location previous to tiptoeing down the path leading to where she stood.

The voice corrected her by telling her, it was not up there on the bridge, it was down beneath the bridge with her. She sarcastically thought how great it was she was not alone anymore. Her new companion was a tiny, invisible voice.

CHAPTER 14

Stone By Stone

A second unseen voice made a remark similar to the first voice about how someone had done well mastering their likeness. Bea worried her stress from losing everyone was making her imagine voices for friends.

The tinier voice seemed to move from up to down, however, the larger sizzing sounding voice was motionless.

Searching the ground around her feet, claws and paws, the confused wee bear saw no one. When the tiny voice informed the larger one Bea couldn't see them, there was a sudden movement in the grass to the right of the startled bear.

How could a voice bend grass? She wondered what invisible creature could wiggle around and speak. It reminded her of the investigation exercises Scruffles and Sweet Puppy conducted with her in their attempt to figure out what the mist monster was.

It turned out, Doolie was another bear mom with all kinds of puppies. There was no reason, after all, for her fears to grow. The mysterious creature ended up becoming a great group of friends.

It occurred to Bea, maybe the voices could belong to potential friends. Her excited wee bear eyes plaintively searched the ground where the movement originated.

Doing her brain exercise, the curious bear realized why she hadn't been able to see the source of the larger voice. Her newfound friend blended with or was as we call it, camouflaged the same color as the grass.

She experienced great joy as she concluded that yes, there was a great likeness. She wondered where the other friend might be. Maybe she was tinier, just like her voice.

She asked her friend whom she named Snakely where the little voice came from and who it belonged to. Spidie zipped down and dangled in front of Bea's nose. There were proper introductions, closing with Bea exclaiming how pleased she was meeting both of them.

Bea's new friends who began with a shadow of one and now three continued to discuss what a great likeness to them was on the large rock across the brook. If they were going to see Bea's likeness, they would have to cross the brook.

As your narrator, I will explain to you, they were discovering a magnificent petroglyph created by the stone pilers or Native Americans of long ago. This consisted of carved artwork or natural paints or charcoal used on stone. Petroglyphs can be found all over the world, if you want to research them.

Bea wanted greatly to know what they were talking about, but had no intention of crossing in that swift current. When she objected, both of her fresh friends laughed.

They explained they were not laughing at her, because true friends would never do that. They further explained they had previously thought the same thing, that the only way across was through the water. Although, Spidie saved the day.

Able to safely travel higher, Spidie saw what Snakely would never have been able to see. There were stones to cross little by little. When Bea heard those familiar words, she knew this was a message from the maker to cross, step by step, stone by stone.

Bea danced in her heart and soul to once again be a member of a team, discussing how reaching the opposite bank would take place. Neither Snakely nor Spidie thought they would be able to stay on wet stones long enough without washing into the river.

Bea did her talk to the maker of spiders, snakes, and wee bears practicing her brain exercise. Snakely was insulted when Bea admitted she'd heard of deceptive sneaky snakes who asked for a ride and even though they promised not to bite their carrier, bit them with a mean bite.

With that unpleasant matter out of the way, next came the question of where Spidie would ride. Spidie suggested, as lookout, she'd take the highest point, which would be the ears, belonging to Bea.

What a delightful sight, a bear with a grass green snake on her right shoulder and a glistening dew spider on her left ear, little by little, step by step, stone by stone crossing a full roaring, white, foaming river.

They were relieved to know when solid ground was beneath Bea's paws, claws and feet. Because they were approaching the rock from a different direction than she'd been standing, Bea stopped in mid-step. She felt faint with chills running all the way through her whole being.

She had the answer to her lagging question of why the maker had wanted her to take risks in climbing down that dreaded hill, step by step, little by little and in making new friends.

CHAPTER 15

A Cry For Help

BOTH SNAKELY and Spidie were mesmerized by their likenesses on the boulder. Bea inquired if either knew who would have made them. They were magnificent. There in front of her were several drawings with her likeness.

Snakely let herself slide down from Bea's right shoulder to the rock surface. Spidie dropped down as on a rope. They felt better situated to be able to make conversation. Moving toward the front, they would have puffed up with joyful pride if possible. There, on the face of the rock, were the distinct drawings of Snakely and Spidie.

They even had Spidie's beautiful web work featured. Although Bea once again asked if either had heard any stories of who could have drawn these, she did have her suspicions.

Her guesses were confirmed when Snakely mentioned she had heard it was longer ago than most could remember. Spidie announced she'd heard it was before the caves her parents' parents decorated.

Bea told them she called them stone pilers because where she and Doolie had their cave, there were many stones piled in a special pattern. Both Snakely and Spidie recalled playing around them.

Chippies would play hide and seek in and out of the holes in the walls between the piled stones. Snakely would zip through them, unless Spidie had been doing her wonderful web work, covering the holes.

Both Chippie and Snakely would get a face full of webs. Spidie couldn't help snickering a tiny bit at that description. Though they had a delightful day, Bea was aware it was time she continued her journey as the maker was directing her.

Neither Snakely nor Spidie had any further plans when Bea offered them a ride, so they accepted and resumed their previous position.

Bea thanked them for being her new friends. She explained how her best friends had all gone to the bridge of rainbows, and they were the first true friends she'd met since then. She did of course add in about wonderful Willow.

Bea wondered why she heard a sizzing snicker coming from her right shoulder, and a tiny teehee coming from her left ear. She was brought back to her painful memories of the little mean bears who used to laugh at her.

This time, rather than feeling hurt and wanting to hide, she simply asked what they were laughing about. She was puzzled at their answer.

They both claimed they found it difficult to make friends because so many were afraid of them and would hide under a rock or behind a tree.

It saddened Bea to hear them tell of times some animals would rather crash or splash into a deep, dangerous river than to stop to consider being friends.

Despite the noisy nonsensical bantering between Spidie and Snakely, Bea did her brain exercise. Occasionally tuning into what was going on with them, she caught Spidie claiming dibs on the highest point, Bea's ears.

The tickling sensation informed Bea, Spidie was hopping from one ear to the other. She laughed as she wondered what Spidie would capture in her ear web. Whatever it was, it would be more friends catching a ride.

Snakely reassured Spidie, there was no competition coming from her for any high spot. She spent her life on the ground and was not like her cousins who nonchalantly climbed trees.

If we could see Bea, we'd notice a look of concern change to a wide smile as she overheard Snakely confess she felt quite comfortable on Bea's shoulder. She judged it to be a fairly smooth ride, and appreciated Bea's assistance.

Silliness between Snakely and Spidie did not prevent Bea doing her notice exercise. Just in time, she saw a puppy get thrown into a car.

Due to its growling, Bea judged it didn't know the person putting her in. Peering through the window with sad eyes, the abducted puppy yelped.

On a vital mission, she cuts through the woods, following the car as it grows smaller. The trail ends near a gray house and unpainted barn, a dark blue car with many dents blocks her clear view to know for sure where the puppy is being kept.

Bea asks Spidie and Snakely to listen to see if they can hear what she hears. It is muffled yet not an unfamiliar sound. She just can't identify where it is coming from.

She is suddenly saddened and troubled to be reminded of the same frantic calling for help she heard when Sweet Puppy had fallen into a hole too deep to climb out of.

Having learned in the past, how to follow Sweet Puppy's voice yelping, signaling she was trapped and in danger, Bea follows the howling they all are hearing, until she spots a wooden barn in the distance. That is the source of the begging for liberation.

CHAPTER 16

Snakely And Spidie Help

THE PLEADING cry, made it clear, the puppy couldn't break free. Bea began scanning and planning, something she was working little by little to stop. With a history of getting into other friends' business she wanted to be especially alert. That obsessive behavior had often led to guilty, and possibly resentful feelings.

Practicing her talk to the maker exercise convinced her she was doing the right thing. She hadn't needed any assistance from her friends, Snakely and Spidie, before, this was new, their assistance would surely be needed this time.

They were going to have to plan together and work as a team, just as Scruffles, she, and Sweet Puppy had on many occasions. In this case someone was expressing a cry for help. She had to admit she could not pull this off on her own. It felt strange to have to consider asking Snakely and Spidie for their aid.

The resolute wee bear was changing her pattern of when to offer help, and practice being humble exercise and ask for help. Though there was a note of urgency in the frenetic barking, she had to do her investigation exercise, joined by her two passengers, Snakely on her shoulder and Spidie on a web between her ears.

Realizing the frantic cries meant, it was possible the puppy knew something Bea did not. This called for alertness and stealth. The one who could speedily slither over to the barn was Snakely.

The first step of the mission was to have Snakely, who would sweetly sidle closer, to see if she could gain more intel, before they planned their approach. Snakely was excited to assist as scout, while Spidie maintained her look out position.

Even with Spidie upon her perch, she could not follow Snakely to locate her in the tall grass. She was hidden and looked just like the grass, until it grew shorter and she could see wiggling blades. She lost Snakely again as she slid beneath the side barn door.

The smart snake chose not to go through the open door so as not to be seen. Spidie and Bea were anxious about Snakely's safety. The two continued to keep their eyes and attention fixed upon Snakely's point of entry.

There was a rustling in the grass beside Bea's feet, paws and claws. Unlike the first time the startled wee bear sucked her breath in as she experienced the tickling sensation, this time there was a sigh of relief.

Bea became aware she'd been holding her breath an unusually long period of time. She breathed more easily as Snakely gave her report. It seems the puppy's name was Lady, and she'd been grabbed by a cruel man and thrown into the barn.

He had muttered something about the van would be here to get her, and he'd be rich. She told Snakely she had no idea what that meant, but it did not bode well for Lady. It was imperative they extricate her immediately.

If Bea's ground plan did not go as hoped, Snakely had a fail-safe counter plan. This would ensure pure distraction for the van man, so everyone could safely drop out of the van driver's sight.

She was going to make her way over to the truck, unlatch the door, then lift all of the locking levers on the crates. That man would have more than Lady to worry about.

This was Bea's original strategy. Spidie would be doing her magic designing an entire curtain of webs covering the entire doorway. Snakely would sequester herself under the doorway.

When the van driver was dragging or carrying Lady out of the barn, heading toward his van, Snakely would raise herself so as to trip up the captor.

That's what he deserved for trying to send dogs on an unnecessary path to the bridge of rainbows. As luck would have it, things became even more tangled for him.

The master plan went off without a hitch. Bea hid behind a wide tree while fate was carried out. It turned out he had long hair under his cap, bushy eyebrows, a long mustache and a broad beard and glasses.

What an ordeal he was in for, his glasses were more gummed up than his eyebrows. With stuck up hair, beard and mustache, he maneuvered with great difficulty, but messed up glasses was another issue. Fumbling for a bandanna to futilely do something about his worthless glasses, his focus changed from Lady to self-survival.

He dropped any contact with Lady and stumbled around attempting to right himself so as not to tumble onto the stone embedded driveway. He could be heard mumbling something about how that would be the clincher, if he were to go down for the count.

CHAPTER 17

The Get Away

THE MESSED-UP dogcatcher worried about the level of embarrassment if anyone were watching. He couldn't see if the man who hired him to capture the dog in the barn was staring out his window or not. With his clownish antics, was he just a pathetic amusement?

Because she'd met Lady, Snakely held greater disgust for the situation than Bea and was committed to do something about it. For Lady's sake, Snakely insisted upon releasing the crated captives in the van. The hesitant mom to her new friends, consented.

Bea wished the fifty swarming bees making a loud buzzing fuss would go to sleep. She wondered what snoring bees would sound like, especially inside her tummy.

How she wished she had her "be good to myself" treat. That would surely quiet the bees. She would be able to better do her "be calm" exercise.

This brought her thoughts to Timothy the Beaver who fashioned those honey pots. So as not to break any, she would use conscious caution, while lifting the clay jars up and down from the shelves as she did her stepstooling exercise. There would be no more if she dropped them all.

She promised herself she would take extra good care of the furniture he had carved for her, also. The list included her stepstool and her cupboard lovingly holding her "be good to myself" treat.

She was unnecessarily stirring the fifty bees, as she worried about something that might never happen. Her brain exercise would sometimes get scrambled like an egg dropped from the nest on the limb of a tree of her friend Dovely.

Her anxious thoughts went from, with no more clay pots to keep the golden honey in them, there would be no place to keep her "be good to myself" treat. With no "be good to myself" treat, she might forget how to be good to herself.

She would have to dig way back to when her mom said she was a good wee bear. Somewhere in the darkness of the forest below and of her thoughts, she remembered to do her talk to the maker about her fears.

She spotted just the right path for them to take off downward as soon as Snakely returned from her self-appointed assignment to create chaos.

It wasn't long before the comedic scene played out.

Realizing his captive dogs were escaping, the van driver was unable to take any action without removing his glasses, leaving him at a greater disadvantage.

His preoccupation with attempting to clear away all of Spidies' excellent entanglements was enough distraction enabling them to escape into the woods. This was a great deception, with him presuming everyone would stick to the pavement.

Bea led all her new charges down the trail deeper into the woods. The bright globe in the sky was concealed by trees, leaves and bows. Without the light of day, it became extremely, nearly impossible for the now mom of many, to find her way. She needed to do her pretend exercise, lest anyone know how lost they might be.

She hoped Snakely and Spidie didn't sense any lack of sureness due to her shaking. She did not want them hearing the rapid thrumming drum beat of her heart. Bea worried they might at least be able to hear the buzzing of confused bees in her tummy.

Settled upon her ears and shoulder, they probably were far enough away from her tummy. Practicing her be calm exercise, she was consoled they could hear nothing. She masked her sense of insecurity.

With that helpful routine exercise, a glowing light shown within, giving her the solution. No longer entertaining her panicky thoughts, she realized there would be some containers of honey somewhere. They could easily be fetched in the dumpster area Doolie told her about.

This was not the time to rehash a dilemma greater than any she'd faced since. Her thoughts were drawn back to when she, Sweet Puppy, and Scruffles had a horrible time finding the path to some targeted dumpsters. Though ending up in a river, they were spared harm when they landed at Timothy's Pond.

After they found a drier route, they experienced further frustration, finding which dumpster of three was the right one. Eventually, there were several more containers filled with her "be good to myself" treat.

With the 50 bees within her, settling down, our inventive bear wondered why she needed to have something to worry constantly. Her rambling thoughts almost always carried her to the worst of times.

After doing her talk with the maker of solutions, she reflected upon her past dilemmas and had to celebrate the fact she had coped, made it through those difficult times and had survived.

Becoming more aware of things around her, she noticed the glowing light was still there!

CHAPTER 18

The Bird With The Guiding Light

THIS IS not a light from her imagination nor a result from doing her talk to the maker. Her mom had taught her about those situations, when she did her brain exercise. This is real and it is coming from above. Strangely, there is no sound accompanying it.

The protective mom of many, needed to practice her investigation exercise to figure out what was emitting that light. The unusual fact about this brightness emanating from above the tree tops was its eerie silence. No humans could be heard yelling or discussing plans to capture or hurt the animals.

The source did not seem to be a blinding search light, looking for Bea and her new buddies, the escaped puppies. The guiding light remained long enough for Bea to step cautiously into the opposite path they were heading. She was receiving a strong message to follow. For some reason, something wanted the skeptical bear to trust it.

Resuming her steps away from the snoring and mewling of the traumatized puppies, she was able to hear and see a brook. She hoped her new charges were like her dear Sweet Puppy who relished the sharp taste of river fish. That was all there would be for the present. Even if it might not have been their favorite, they were probably hungry enough to want to gobble up anything swimming.

The mysterious light hovering like a humming bird that could stay in one place and not crash to the ground, remained long enough for Bea to roust everyone and guide them to the river. She explained they would be safe and fed if they wanted to grab some fish swimming among the rocks.

This happiness and relief reminded her of the music the pebbles made as they gently or not so gently tapped each other, singing their stories. The ability to see her surroundings helped the proud mom bear to notice what fun everyone was having.

It made her think of the first time she saw Sweet Puppy having fun. She figured this was the first time some of those sad puppies had ever had that much time to play.

In addition to the bright bird guiding her to the river, it revealed an easy path for them to follow. As the light began to move more toward the path, the curious bear wondered if the giant bird was going to lead them the whole way.

She did her talk to the maker of giant silent birds with lights. She needed to know if she should trust it. Hearing the reassuring humming of the kind bees that made her "be good to herself treat, told her she could safely follow the huge bird.

The bird led them to a place they could be safe, and it wasn't a wooden building like the one where the humans with harmful black sticks hurt her cousins.

The final location the bird directed them toward was to a roomy cave situated in the side of a grassy hill, with tiny rivulets of fresh water trickling down from a mountain.

Bea was conflicted when she did her notice exercise. There were enough spacious chambers for everyone to comfortably reside. Possibly no one would want to continue their trek. She'd be alone again.

Taking her mind off herself, Bea was wondering where the bird would go, since they had been delivered to a secure destination. All would be able to remain hidden from any dangerous humans.

Just as the appreciative wee bear was hoping to be able to thank the bird, it began to move, ever higher, showing colors of the garden of flowers her mom had pointed out to her as a child.

The bird of many flower-colored blinking lights rose until it was a tiny speck. Bea's eyes grew as large as the light above as it flew faster than any bird she had ever known of. Then it was gone.

A bit dazed, she turned around toward their new temporary home. Spidie would consider that an ideal spot to be the lookout for everyone. Both she and Snakely had been exceptionally quiet for some time.

The web making genius announced she would consider it an honor to be the lookout for such a large group. She declared with pride to Bea and Snakely what a respectable responsibility it would be. It occurred to Bea neither Snakely nor Spidie ate fish.

Snakely reported she and Spidie had become even closer. She proudly announced the two of them had again worked together as a team, for a different purpose, this time. Bea soon found out why.

Spidie hopped around, becoming increasingly animated when Snakely complimented Spidie for building a perfect web to capture a large number of delicious juicy bugs. Bea was unaware Spidie was sharing her exquisite catch with Snakely.

CHAPTER 19

What Was vs What Can Be

BEA LAUGHED to herself at the thought her head should have felt light when Spidie had only begun building a web with a connection between her right and left ear. She hadn't noticed the increase in weight as Spidie added to the catch.

A sense of weightlessness would eventually result as they delighted in their 'be good to themselves' treat.

Leaving her flights of fancy of thought, she turned her attention toward more serious matters. She wondered how many would follow her on her next stroll of discovery.

Would they choose to begin again using her new technique of little by little? Or would they prefer to remain in the concealed, secure dwelling the magnificent bird led them to.

Bea was not surprised, nevertheless, saddened when everyone, including Snakely and Spidie chose to remain with the puppies. There was plenty of food for everyone.

This would be a good spot for them to stay until, like tree limbs, they would slowly branch out in the different directions they felt called toward. Once again, sadly, she surrendered her responsibility as a mom.

With a good rest, sure the maker had more in store for her, Bea knew it was necessary to continue on her journey. An opportunity was presenting itself, to choose between what was or what can be. At an earlier time, Willow had suggested the searching wee bear focus on beginning again.

In preparation for her launch out onto the next leg of her itinerary, the hungry bear needed the sustenance of the fish the others had dined upon. She backtracked to the fishing river. As Bea stepped into the rippling waters, she became aware of a stream of tears cascading off her nose.

It was a healing of letting go of her losses, confusion and self-doubt. The dear wee bear stood there sobbing until she felt finished. Relieved, her emotions had been freed by the comforting embrace of the swirls of the current, she was readying to take the next step.

Just as the rivulets of sparkling spring waters began somewhere up higher, she knew the maker was guiding her to the action of beginning again. She had learned much and had helped many to begin again, but this was not yet, her time.

Bea would ordinarily be in her cave home doing her stepstooling exercise to enjoy her "be good to myself" treat. Surely, it was time for some golden goodness to appear. She would love such a sticky surprise. She wished she could be going up and down the stepstool carved by her dear friend Timothy the beaver.

Recognizing, that as an unreachable goal, she settled for the food of her baby kitty, Scruffles and Sweet Puppy. She smiled as she remembered how her two little ones had believed they were doomed to a life of catching and eating the same boring fish.

As we know, their menu changed radically, after hunting down and meeting Doolie, another wise bear, and her crew. You may remember or are being told the story for the first time. Doolie, a dear friend, tipped Bea off to a secret place to collect exquisite foods for Scruffles and Sweet Puppy.

She told Bea it was called a dumpster and was located at the rear of some stores. Bea sadly smiled as she remembered the dumpster diving disaster. Back then, if her two buddies, Scruffles and Sweet Puppy had not rescued her, she would still be trapped in one of those dumpsters.

From harsh experiences, that bear who had been fooled too many times, had become a dumpster connoisseur. However, for now, she'd have to catch some fresh river fish. To distract her tastebuds from the fishiness, she focused on the wise tree, Willow and her favorite phrase, 'little by little.' That was how Bea was to stroll to find her next important discovery, to begin again.

After leaving the wooded section of the puppy cave home, Bea strolled in an area she'd never been. She was aware of being alone once again, except for her dark-colored dancing friend, we would call a shadow. The anticipating bear looked forward to seeing her when she showed herself in the bright times.

Bea was unable to estimate how far she'd strolled. But her feet, claws and paws knew. She had no idea where she was going, but was certain where she'd been. The time had come to adjust her mood and outlook, to begin again.

Skidding to a stop to rest the pads of her feet, she began looking around to do her notice exercise. As she did her talk to the maker of tired wee bears who walked too long a distance, she felt strange, yet wonderful.

A breeze stirred. Something had changed within her, causing her to perceive her surroundings differently. Searching the region, Bea found no mountains nearby, yet the echoes of the birds' chattering fascinated her.

Brighter colors could be seen in the broad sky with designs of purples, blues, and pinks, no human being could ever create. The singing leaves were in tune with various birds. Bea felt in tune with what could be.

CHAPTER 20

Renewed

THROUGHOUT THIS entire performance, Dovely was 'who-who-who- ing' in a dance rhythm. Brilliant rose-red cardinals exchanged different notes. Branches clicked together, keeping time. The wee mesmerized bear stilled herself.

Taking it all in, ancient tones wove in and through her, strengthening the feeling of being a part of the sights and sounds. She remained in that state for some time, doing her brain exercise, feeling the maker, surrounding her with protection.

It was glorious, until came the nudge from the maker of searching bears. It was time to proceed, to learn to begin again. Bea did not fully understand the reason for the directive, but followed it anyway. The maker had not let her down yet.

She sensed a tear or two, sliding down her muzzle. They were tears of joy for the gift of the outstanding experience she'd just had. She was also weeping tears of sadness, to have to leave such a place of safety.

Renewed and filled with hope, our dear wee bear was certain things could only get better. Elated, Bea danced and hummed a tune of happiness. Imitating some of these delightful sounds surrounding her, carried her back to the sensation of being wrapped in a blanket of comfort.

Because everyone was at the bridge of rainbows, she and Willow the counseling tree had talked about her needing to branch out in her strolling exercises. She wasn't certain if the spectacle her eyes beheld was real or part of the dreamy gift she still carried in her heart.

Nonetheless, she was convinced she spied an occupied cave. There were logs and branches piled near the entrance. Someone had clearly worked to collect the curious pile.

The wee bear shuffled closer, remembering the polite ways her mom taught her. Not desiring to alarm anyone, she gently approached the mystery home.

Her dancing friend, who made, never a sound, would not create any disturbance. Checking to see if her hide-and-seek friend was still there, Bea was startled to notice her friend had doubled. One dark figure stood right beside the other.

She quickly did her brain exercise. Neither Snakely nor Spidie had a friend like hers who danced. So, she wondered whose friend was standing beside hers. As she turned to do her investigation exercise, jaws wide open, a totally stunned Bea, stood there.

Her wee bear heart stood still. She wondered if this was the end of her search. Was this where the maker of bears and old bear friends had led her? Her long lonely stroll with no answers finally had come to a conclusion, and to an end.

She remembered Willow had said searchers sometimes have to carry the question until it is time to lay it down, to hold the answer in their paws. Tiny rivulets of tears ran down her muzzle with an accompanying runny nose as she reflected upon how long she'd carried that question which had wearied, discouraged and frustrated her.

The question, a familiar companion, had grown in size and weight. Bea felt she might crumble under its load, but dared not put it down. Her all too well-known 'what-if's' were splashing around in her head like river fish. Restless bees were growing in number throughout her tummy. She feared the answer to the question she'd been grappling with, was not in front of her.

Billie bear knew who Bea was at the moment Bea recognized her old friend. Even with time having passed, since they last saw each other, with the heart memory each had for the other, recognition, would be immediate.

When they had seen nineteen long, dark snows, the duo joined a group of other bears. Their moms reluctantly remained in their cave homes while the two young adventurers left their safety and guidance.

If bears could smile and hug, we'd see those two longtime friends, hopping up and down hugging with big smiles on their faces. Billie Bear was becoming tangled around Jazzy, her dancing puppy, and Bea had to steady herself as she was ready to tumble along with Billie bear into the high grass.

They joyfully laughed as they whirled with excitement, both playfully tumbling to the soft lush ground. Billie Bear had to caution her puppy to calm down for a moment. He was about to meet Bea the wee bear, her old best friend about whom she had often told him.

The two ecstatic bears were interrupting each other as they somberly reminisced about the group they had been in together. Its existence was known by many bears like their moms, who had survived many more cold times with iced-up trees, than their young daughters, Billie Bear and Bea. However, little other information was provided.

They had mixed feeling but knew this is what their daughters believed they wanted. The moms loved them enough to risk letting them go.

They were, however, puzzled their little ones wanted to leave their comfortable cave homes to join a group with less than adequate living conditions.

CHAPTER 21

Billie Bear

THEY MET at the fork in the pebble covered dirt road. Both Bea and Billie bear, a dear friend from such a long time ago, were excited to get there to meet the new group of special bears. They were going to be learning how to talk better to the maker.

Billie had always had a better sense of direction than Bea. They would have surely gotten lost, if it were left to Bea to follow up on directions given them.

These thoughts brought her back to how her mom told her this frequently becoming lost happened was because she held her purple crayon with the opposite paw from most bears she knew.

Having taken sufficient twists around this tree, turns toward that bush, and having climbed enough hills, the travelers knew they were nearing the specified location.

It was like an outdoor umbrellaed school for humans, except it was bears being taught by other bears. With the lovely setting of tall pines wafting invigorating scents, who would not want to be there?

The group had many bears who appeared as old as their moms. They told each other they hoped this was going to be as an enriching experience as it looked like.

As the lovely leaves began to flutter to the ground, doing her notice exercise, Bea became sharply aware of something. There was a feeling around her unlike when she was with her mom.

With continuous encouragement she could learn and experiment with new ways to accomplish a task. These older bears criticized many things Bea did when carrying out assigned duties. They complained she was neither fast enough nor thorough enough.

She was tiring of hearing how things have always been done. How could this bullying be happening again in Bea's life? She was no longer a cub, but a fully grown bear.

She speculated maybe previously; older unhappy bears bullied these bears when they were novices. Many present bullies were bullied at an earlier time in their lives. Possibly that's why some of the older bears in the group were bullying the two newbies.

Bea did not know bullies could be old. She thought only little bears could be mean. Some of those older bears spoke as if they had the black stinging bees coming out of their mouths. Feeling like the swarm headed directly for her, brought back memories of the little mean bears, she thought she'd left behind.

Fortunately, for Billie Bear, only a few stopped to zing her. The two fresh-to-the-earth learners were enchanted with the opportunity to be a part of a group studying how to do the talk to the maker exercise.

Their enthusiasm faded like a bright flame dimming for lack of fuel. This attitude and treatment of them disappointed and confused the well brought up bears. What they were experiencing went against everything their moms had taught them.

A few kind bears in the group did explain everything to the nervous newcomers. They reported they had had a difficult time when first joining the group, but in turn found some older ones who treated them decently. This process was much like moms teaching their cubs to teach their little ones. Or as we say, 'passing it forward.'

Eventually, Billie Bear had had enough, seeing no purpose for remaining, left the group. Even though she was happy for Billie Bear making a difficult choice, Bea missed her.

She stayed longer to see if she could learn more from those she looked up to. Her primary purpose and dream were to teach some of the older bears the exercises her mom had taught her.

In spite of difficult times, there was another reason for remaining. She wanted to teach about her "be good to myself" treat. She had hopes they might feel better about themselves and be nicer to others.

They could learn to do the notice exercise, to become aware of things around them, rather than focus only on themselves. Learning to listen to the rhythm of rocks in the streams, they would hear the songs of the waters.

If they could listen to the music of the chanting winds as they skipped through the leaves and branches, their hearts would be lighter. They might discover hope. Instead, it seemed they preferred to remain grumpy and unhappy.

Bea wondered why, even if they had all kinds of opportunities to change their way of looking at things, some animals were more content to be unhappy. Doing her brain exercise didn't even help make the matter clearer. This was another question whose answer she wasn't sure she'd ever uncover.

Bea sensed a great apathy, with no expression of desire to learn the exercises she so dearly wanted to teach them. Their lack of interest and stubbornness broke Bea's heart. She found it difficult to understand how they could be in a group learning to talk to the maker, but didn't act like it.

After Bea finally gave up, Billie bear and she got together to compare stories. The two fully intended to remain in touch, however, situations changed, as they do for all of us. In the meantime, Bea became preoccupied with her new charges, Scruffles and Sweet Puppy, and invited them to live with her in the roomy cave home.

Bea told Billie bear, when she met Doolie and her crew, her whole life opened up. Bea began sobbing before she could even get another word out. Taking deep breaths, she was too choked up.

CHAPTER 22

Osala Bear

BETWEEN GREAT gasps, Bea told her dear friend, Billie bear, about her many companions who had stepped onto the path of the bridge of rainbows. Billie bear didn't realize, until then, how greatly things had changed for both of them.

She had a collection in her heart of dear friends who had also traveled to the bridge of rainbows. The one she missed the most was her partner for life. He had been wonderful and the best thing to happen for her.

As both of them wept, drawing closer, Bea recited what Willow had told her about how there needed to be tears on our cheeks to feel the rainbow in our hearts. This saying had comforted her and she hoped the same for Billie bear.

Bea reported presently there were no other heartbeats in her cave, except for some spidies and a mouse or two. Billie bear heartily agreed it was important to have a companion or two and that was why she had Jazzy, her precious puppy, living in her cave home.

As things are ever-changing in our lives, Billie bear announced having a very new occupant in the back of her cave whom she hoped Bea would like to meet and invite to be that heartbeat she so needed to have beside her in her dark, hollow, hallow cave.

Bea did not expect this news. She wondered what the maker was up to, but smiled in her heart, knowing this could be the answer she was seeking. Nevertheless, it would be the answer best for her.

Billie bear told the story of how her friend Osala bear and her kitty little Osala were enjoying a walk in a people's park with picnic tables. They frequently visited this ideal area to find delicacies to munch on.

Osala kitty's favorite was the tuna sandwiches dropped or thrown under the picnic tables. When it looked as if someone had come through, cleaning up any scraps of food, they meandered over to an out of the way, undiscovered section of tables.

There was a body of water nearby with gravelly ground leading to the picnic table. Checking to see if there were any other occupants, they approached the closest table. Peering beneath, Little Osala was the first to see it.

When her mom investigated, she observed there were actually several. They discussed how they could carry them. They usually ate on the spot, what they discovered, never with a need to carry anything.

This was a unique situation, with a daunting task. Little Osala's stare was fixed on her remarkable find. Her mom double-checked to see if there was any life left there. As she got closer there seemed to be only one still stirring.

The medium-sized kitty lying there weakly whispered his concern, his two sisters and mother were too quiet. They'd neither spoken nor moved. He felt alone, as we would say abandoned. He did not understand they had left for the bridge of rainbows.

After Osala explained the situation to little Osala she reached out to gently lift the sad kitty and tell him he would be all right. She explained she was going to take him to her cave home and briefly introduced herself and little kitty Osala.

Respecting his need to sleep, neither spoke on the hike home. Both likely had many questions, hopes and apprehensions. Osala set him carefully onto the soft cedar boughs. The two of them watched him as he slept, wondering what frightening experiences he had lived through in his short life.

His gentleness and preciousness were overshadowed by his vulnerability, which led to defensiveness. Sadly, it was not long before Osala's certainty about the outcome of this short-lived stay grew. Being a protective mom, this stranger to her, would not be able to stay long.

The newly discovered kitty acted as if he were the boss of Osala and kitty Osala's cave home. He was bullying little Osala so much, mom Osala was worried he might seriously harm her. That would not do.

She asked kind-hearted Billie bear if she could take him. It seemed it would work out. She was mom to her puppy Jazzy who was slightly larger than the smaller frightened, on-edge kitty.

It was a good thing Billie bear had an extensive cave and fortunately was strong. Having to separate them into two different cave rooms, far from each other, called for lifting and lugging short logs to attempt to make a wall of safety for Jazzy.

However, this adept climber and hunter, bolted over the wooden wall built to block him. His oppressive presence was soon made known to a jumbled Jazzy who was sure the intimidator would attack. Our list of self-defenders grows longer. As with Scruffles, Sweet Puppy, Annie, and Stormy, Jazzy made ready to be zinged.

CHAPTER 23

Wounded Moms

BEFORE THE aggressor had time, to rear up, Jazzy, was ready. A violent, raucous cat and dog fight ensued. The mom of her favorite dear Jazzy, and the newly abandoned one, was torn.

Our list of wounded moms also grows longer. Buddy bear and Stormy must have done all of the right things. Buddy bear is not on our list. However, Billie bear joins the group at the top.

Bea had noted a slight limp as Billie Bear gave her the tour. She soon found out its source was none other than the same ordeal taking Doolie and her down. Attempting to break up a fight. Are we seeing a pattern here?

Billie Bear made the same mistakes as Bea and Doolie had. You may remember Bea's tales of being scratched, bitten, and almost drown when her two, Scruffles and Sweet Puppy fought. Doolie got bitten by Sweet Puppy by accident, when she, Annie and Zoe were fighting.

As the ungrateful, invited guest began to scratch and bite Jazzy, Billie Bear wanted to rescue her puppy and to put a stop to all of the fighting. She seriously wondered how this was all going to work out when she got severely wounded on her foot while attempting to yank the raucous raccoon cat off her puppy, Jazzy.

Rather than an attempted slash toward, Jazzy, the paws with seriously lethal cat claws missed their mark. Instead, at least three dangerous claws seemed to eject at lightning speed, making contact with Billie Bear's left foot.

Billie bear informed Bea she had come to her mind, as a solution, but wasn't sure what cave she was in and with whom she was living. Bea immediately knew this little creature was the maker's answer to her search for someone to share her cave home.

Billie Bear cautioned her it would not be easy. Another problem was that he basically refused to chew anything. He claimed he did not have dog teeth. Hearing this curt report alerted Bea she was going to have to do some serious searching around or in, the dumpsters.

The one positive aspect for him living with Bea, was there would be no one for this rowdy raccoon cat to fight with. He would be able to have his own spot, and would not have to share it or a mom. He would no longer require enclosure behind any barriers.

This thought comforted Billie bear and gave her enough courage to inquire if her friend might take such a rebellious cat. Upon further inquiry, Bea discovered this poor fellow had not been given a permanent name yet.

You may remember, Bea wants everyone to have a name so if they ever needed help, the maker could find them immediately. She decided she'd name him Sammy. The name seemed to fit him. His approval was obvious.

Called by that name, he came leaping, being rewarded with a 'be good to himself' treat Billie Bear had for him. He reminded Bea of Zoe, one of the puppies who had lived with Doolie, Bea's best friend, before one horrible event after another revealed itself.

The reflective bear, took time to do her brain exercise. Having lived with Zoe gave her an idea of the complications she might face with Sammy. Zoe was particular about what she ate.

Doolie found hotdogs for her in the dumpsters we've heard about. It didn't sound like Sammy was going to be chewing on any hotdogs, or chicken as found by Sweet Puppy back then.

She wondered if he'd like the tuna Scruffles always joyfully found for himself. That made her think she needed to clue mom Osala in to finding tuna for little Osala at the dumpsters. That would be a courtesy her mom had continuously reminded her of as she found ways to thank neighbors for their kindnesses.

Bea could hear Willow's words encouraging her to take a risk, something difficult for her. It dawned on her, she could build a friendship with him, little by little. It all flashed back, the terrible mistake she'd made with Scruffles and what she learned as they had to begin again to form a bond.

She was already planning an outing where Sammy could seek the food he favored. She'd frequently noticed torn bags with a cat on it, seeming to enjoy the food. Hopefully, Sammy could find the same bag.

She was doing her pretend exercise and picturing him with a similar satisfied smile as the cats on the bag. She wasn't even certain he'd follow. The fact she would promise there was something special for him at the end of their trek might be a plan.

CHAPTER 24

The Mystery Bag

BEA MOVED from doing her pretend exercise to her brain exercise and finally to her talk to the maker of forsaken kitties. She turned to Billie bear and told her she would joyfully welcome Sammy as a new family member.

Billie bear gave a grateful bear hug, relieved she and Jazzy could get back to their calm routine. When Jazzy realized what was happening, he yipped and danced for joy. It was a dance of release, of being free from threat of harm or attack.

Seeing Jazzy doing a celebrative romp, reminded her she had not danced unless she saw a rainbow. Her dear friends were signaling her from the bridge of rainbows that everyone had been reunited.

She was happy for them; however, it was not time to join them, there was still more to her journey. And it lightened her burden to know she would no longer stroll alone. She smiled to know Sammy would be beside her.

Hearing of Sammy's finicky appetite similar to Zoe's, alerted Bea's full awareness she needed to hunt for something special for Sammy, and fast. She brought him along on an escapade to the dumpsters where he could pick out his "be good to himself" treat.

She needed to find a way to give him enough motivation to agree to go along with her. Whatever it was, it worked. Willow had cautioned her if she disliked the one solution she had, it was time to look for another one, and another until she found one that did work.

Since all of the sled dogs were at the bridge of rainbows, Bea assumed the honorary role of a sled dog. What a strange sight that must have been, a bear pulling a sled and a raccoon kitty in tow.

No one was afforded the opportunity to witness the spectacle because cautious Bea planned these trips just before the morning mist formed. Although bears, cats, and dog have adequate night vision, this at times became problematic.

She still set up piles of stones, so they would never lose their way. This was the system she learned ancient stone pilers had created. Since she had used their technique, she never went the wrong way again. She wanted to tell Sammy of the wet failed attempt. But stopped.

He wasn't listening and probably didn't care. He was not going to be interested in her old memories. He was very young. It would take time. With Billie bear warning her to be cautious, it would be necessary to practice the on-guard exercise as her mom had taught her.

The new mom was sad to realize she and Sammy would have to make their own adventures to hold in their hearts to remember. This was the hard part of learning to begin again.

Sometimes she wanted to curl up in a ball. She wished she could walk through an old remembered darkened strolling path and when she came out into a bright clearing, she'd be back with Doolie and her crew along with Scruffles and Sweet Puppy.

Accompanied by his new mom, Sammy, the champion jumping and diving kitty, disappeared into the third dumpster After rustling around inside it, he jumped up, and sat upon the edge with a curious bag of something.

It didn't look like anything he might be interested in. As Bea neared the mystery bag, she had the widest bear grin on her muzzle showing many whites, soon to be golden coated teeth.

That sweet boy, later to be nicknamed such, had found a bag of many twig-sized tubes, filled with honey. His next vault through the air was a rewarding one for him. As he landed on the dumpster cover lid, he spotted the treasured bag of goodies.

Someone had left it outside of the dumpster, so all he had to do was push it off, as kitties are wont to do. It landed hitting its target, the middle of the sled. Unsure when they'd return, the resourceful bear coaxed Sammy onward, hoping he'd find more good stuff for each of them.

Bea was happy for the weightiness of the sled, filled with two almost full torn bags, and three cracked jars nearly brimming with honey. Sammy was justifiably proud and already feeling better about himself. Bea could tell this by his tone and his light-stepping dance.

She wouldn't bother tell him, but Bea couldn't help remembering how she'd gotten the sled and what led up to it. She could still feel the tomatoes and bananas squishing between her toes, claws and paws.

Doolie had directed them to the first dumpster. Counting as her mom had taught her, there were three dumpsters. Impulsively choosing what she thought was the first, turned out to be the third.

The first being the third and the third being the first, did not bode well for Bea. Stepping down into the darkness of the dumpster her feet met some mealy mushy stuff. In an effort at flight, she needed Scruffles to heft her high enough to be able to grab onto the lip of the trapping box.

CHAPTER 25

Foe Or Friend

IT WAS only because of a caring Osala bear's discovery of a kitty all by himself, beneath a picnic table, still alive, that Sammy was with Bea. That was what made the ordeal more painful. There was a slump in the shoulders as Bea slowly moved toward the comforting tree, she named Willow. Emptiness lurked within emptiness.

She wanted Sammy to learn from his mistakes and grow to believe in himself. As Willow would say, she needed to look beyond her problems to solutions. He had to begin learning to be an adult with acceptable characteristics for survival, one being using his words. In the event he was unable to stroll through the trees, down the paths with a variety of things to sniff and investigate there would be trouble.

His behavior became more aggressive as his anger and frustration increased. Bea often had a limp similar to Billie bear, her old-time friend, who befriended him. Both were wounded as a result of Sammy's aggressive action to express his aggravation.

As if it were her fault everything was too wet with water dripping from the saturated leaves of trees overhead! Finding no way to enjoy himself, Sammy lashed out tooth and claw at his unsuspecting mom's leg as if she were a leg of lamb. Contrary to this acting out, moderation & patience were called for. Bea wondered if there were a way to instill a conscience in Sammy.

As she jaggedly managed her way toward Willow's sacred spot, she sucked in her breath and halted. She was so comforted to see Willow was still there. Though the loyal tree had said she'd always be there, Bea usually did one of her infamous 'what-if's.'

As she grew closer, her whole being fluttered with hope. As they discussed Sammy, Willow guided Bea to change the words in her heart from I can't solve this to, can I solve this? to a resolve, I can solve this. She could face this dilemma with help. Willow suggested she introduce a friend to Bea who would be able to understand Sammy better than any others.

However, puzzled she was, about how this could work, she did pay as close attention as possible. A serious distraction made this difficult. Bea was certain Willow was unaware what had just emerged from the thickets, to the right of them. A swallow choked in her dry throat. The busy buzzing bees within were stilled, silent. She did a quick inventory of defense tactics her mom had taught her. None seemed sufficient against this degree of threat.

Bea's mouth opened and closed. No sound could be made. All that might have been heard was a muted whimper. Much like Sammy clawing his way up a tree or Bea's tender leg she didn't want it tearing up Willow's already sufficiently scarred bark,

She found the ability to tear her fixed attention away from the ominous sight. In doing this, she was able to understand what was happening. She was staring at Athena, who was going to be a great companion for Sammy and respite for his beleaguered mom.

Upon hearing this, Bea lowered her head and began weeping. She felt as if a branch with great heaviness on her shoulders was finally lifted. After Willow reassured Bea, Athena was a friendly bobcat, as taught by her mom, Bea cordially introduced herself.

Also, carrying out another tradition, Bea invited Athena to join Sammy and her in their cave home. On their stroll toward Athena's new home, Bea filled her in with all that had been going on with Sammy, in addition to his wild beginnings.

Willow had purposely not told Bea much more about Athena. She knew Bea would grow closer to Athena if she were the one to discover who Athena was. The wise tree had reassured Bea, Athena had been commissioned with a vital project called 'Tame Sammy.' And that she knew Athena was qualified for the task. Bea felt hope for the first time in a while.

As your narrator I will tell you, Native Americans or stone pilers, as Bea named them, trust their secrets to the bobcat spirit. This revealer of truth was going to be a friend and protector to Bea and an excellent support for Sammy. Athena would understand his wildness.

As we know, Bea has one concern whenever she invites anyone to live with her. Athena told Bea she need not worry about her "be good to myself" treat, as Athena dined on mice and fish. Bea told her she knew the best fishing spots. Athena flashed a bobcat smile.

They were already off to a good start. Athena could turn out to be a good friend. Some may remember, Bea's mom long ago told her there were always potential friends to be made. Bea smiled to herself thinking how happy her mom would be for all the courageous growing she was doing.

CHAPTER 26

A Costume Contest

SAMMY APPEARED apprehensive when meeting Athena who glanced at Bea, so she would notice the bobcat knew what she was doing. He also peered at his mom for confirmation Athena was a safe person. Later, Bea told Sammy if he felt uncomfortable with anything Athena asked him to do, to immediately let her know.

When they had more time together, Athena confided to Sammy she was in a Bobcat gang of girls named Cats. The boys' gang was called the Bobs. They used to group up, to find caves or burrow entrances to frighten everyone. She worried Sammy might get caught up in one of those groups because he was so aggressive, violent and hurtful. She explained no one in her group would hurt anyone, but just startle them. But there was one time they were the ones who got more than scared.

Athena described how there was a human around with something made of a kind of brown wooden branch with a black thinner branch coming out of it. Whatever it was, it threw out tiny pebble-like things.

She snarled when she announced they hurt more than pebbles. They stuck right in the body and didn't bounce off like a pebble would.

Athena's voice shook as she told how her friend Pallas had the sharp things sticking in her ribs. Pallas' caring, concerned friend clawed & clawed at the place where those pebbles were sticking in her and finally got it out. It was a strangely shaped object made of material she didn't understand.

Athena tearfully reassured Sammy, after taking a long time to be able to run or breathe right, Pallas was finally okay. Athena made a promise neither of them would go anywhere near the Cats' gang, whether or not they were still gathering to bully anyone.

Bea shuddered as she heard this story. She knew exactly what Athena was referring to. This description of the stick shooting out hurtful pebbles brought her back to the traumatic time she and her mother were searching out good honey trees, where bees made her 'be good to myself' treat.

There was a thunderstorm with jagged lightning. The wooden building where Bea's mom felt they'd be dry and safe turned out to be as if they'd walked into a dark world filled with her relatives who had been targeted for the bridge of rainbows. Yes, she was very aware of what Athena was describing.

Sammy's ears perked up. That was a memory Sammy was interested in learning more about. Athena's story along with his mom's felt like a warning for him. He'd had enough trauma and sufficiently raised the level of chaos for others. He wanted to be done with it all.

Bea was on alert when she heard a great commotion around the front of the dumpster building where she had led everyone for their cache of goodies. She knew she was responsible for two others. Athena and Sammy were harvesting treats from the dumpsters and she hoped they heard nothing to alarm them. Athena was thrilled to find turkey, definitely not on her usual meager menu.

Tiptoeing closer, Bea peeked around the building. She did not rebound soon enough and was spotted by a group of costumed young humans. What would she ever do? She had to warn Athena and Sammy. She couldn't flee, they were already running toward her. She could never harm them. These were children whose stories Willow recounted.

They surrounded her, shouting they had found the winner of the costume contest She was the winner? Their shouting wasn't the hurt feeling of shouts the mean bears used when she was little. They were laughing and dancing too. It wasn't the same kind of laughter of making fun.

She did a little two-step herself. The shouting and laughter actually made Bea feel good. Feeling unexpectedly important, she followed the wave of costumed young ones.

The dazzled wee bear zoomed in on an elegant poodle who introduced herself silently as Sophia the special white Poodle. She could trust Sophia who told her no one knew she was a real Poodle, but believed her to be a tiny human with a great costume.

Bea gathered enough clues to assess she was now the participant of a costume contest. Sophia told her the little humans thought Bea was one of them with the best costume. They were yelling they'd never seen such a great bear costume looking so life-like.

There was a momentary panic when Bea spied all of the steps she would have to climb. How would she do it? It didn't resemble the extremely tall tree she had climbed and safely descended for Timothy her friend the clay pot making, wood carving beaver.

Above the deafening drone of anxious bees within her, she remembered to talk to the maker of steps about her dilemma.

CHAPTER 27

. . . .

A Dear Joyous Wee Bear

CALMING HER thoughts, she was able to do her notice exercise. She realized she'd seen those steps before, just smaller and fewer. She remembered Willows words for her to remember, not how can I or can I but, I can.

Sophie crowned her with a ring of lovely black eyed Susans. One of the older costume clad individuals handed her a prize basket with a large handle. It was announced to her this was for being the only one with the greatest bear costume.

Bea couldn't help scan the contents of her prize, her wee heart was secretly swaying in dance. The best part of the prize was the giant, golden-colored jar containing what Bea called her "be-good-to-myself" treat.

The sun-colored joy was snuffed out when Bea felt a familiar sharp poke. She suddenly felt as young and powerless as she had when the mean little bears used to bully her. Her tears turned from tracks down her furry cheeks, to trembling.

Bea experienced what felt like a mean poke identical to ones she received when she was a young bear being bullied by the mean bears around her. She realized she had identified the poke and was absolutely correct. It was the same poke and it was delivered by the same mean bear.

After all those years, Jabber, who used to poke the hardest, of all the other bears, was up to his same old tricks. He would brag he was poking the blubber on the fat bear. His poke hurt more this time for at least two reasons.

She had vigorously practiced her exercises of stair stepping, toe touching, floor touching, and running in place. All of these exercises were required in weight lifting her pots of honey down from her cupboards Timothy the furniture carving, clay pot making beaver created for her.

Her exercises, especially strolling and doing her talk to the maker had helped her become wee, more trusting in the maker and friends. She not so lonely and independent, but allowing others and the maker to help.

She thought living her life daring to make new friends like Doolie and her crew, Benny, Zoe, Annie, and Maddie, made the bad memories go away. When Bea told Sophia what was happening, she immediately masterminded a plan.

Because Sophia's friend Red could be invisible, she could slip into fur and ears, one...then the other, causing a high-pitched flapping of wee wings. This would cause the old familiar aggressor to switch his focus from Bea to himself. She did not want to go back to having those old feelings of helplessness ever again.

The celebration continued in spite of a flailing pretend kid dressed in a real live bear costume with a ladybug in his ear, the right then the left. Bea, carrying the basket of her "be good to myself" treat, stepped downward on her now recognized giant stair stepper, doing her talk to the maker with each step.

She was greeted by her very recent newly made friends Sammy and Athena. There was a sense of relief she had previously been unaware of. With Athena's help and role modeling, Sammy was shaping up into a respectful, respectable young boy kitty.

She considered the faint possibility that she would not have to send Sammy away to spend time with her loyal friend, Buddy bear. You may remember Buddy bear was a great help when Zoe was out of control. Buddy bear had always worked with troubled animals, mostly puppies but occasionally kitties.

She had previously consulted with Buddy bear in case it was ever necessary for her to work with Sammy on his unacceptable troubled behavior. The new mom was relieved she could tell Buddy bear things were working out after all. She was comforted to know she could keep Buddy bear in mind if things deteriorated.

After she filled her new friends in about the chaotic goings-on with Jabber her longtime ago bully and wonderful Sophia and Red, they danced up and down for joy chanting Sophia and Red's name.

We leave Bea, our dear joyous wee bear, with her old and newly-made friends with great hopes for the future. How can she miss? She now has her sweet boy Sammy who will be her strolling and sleeping companion.

I think we all would agree, Bea the wee bear has shown us how to learn to begin again. Now that she has begun her new life and adventures again, we could say the sky's the limit for her.

She believes that is possible to all as we struggle to begin something again, seeing it come to fruition is a reward for our efforts carried out little by little. Our favorite bear thanks you for joining her in her stroll, searching for answers, little by little. She hopes this has helped you if ever you need to learn to begin again.

We conclude this series of books about Bea the wee bear.

THE END

GLOSSARY

BRAIN EXERCISE
Serious thinking and/or meditation.

STROLLING
Walking with great alertness.

STEPSTOOLING
Going up and down a step stool to get clay pots of honey.

FINE MOTOR WEIGHT LIFTING
Using the paw to lift gobs of honey from the pot to the mouth.

TOE TOUCHING
Not wanting to waste a drop of honey, bending over to earnestly clean the gooey toes.

FLOOR TOUCHING
Similar to toe touching except having to bend over further, to the floor.

BULLY
To taunt, call names, belittle by laughing, exclude from activities, and emotionally pushy, often resulting in long-term trauma and emotional scarring.

NOTICE EXERCISE

Really focus on what is in front of you, to really see things as they are, all done without distraction; a good way to clear the mind.

PLANNING AND SCANNING

A little bit of plotting to figure out how to solve someone's problem that is basically unsolicited, this often ends up badly.

STUCK

Unable to move on; fixated on an idea or situation or problem.

FEARS

A form of anxiety, often resulting from trauma from a painful or frightening incident or bullying.

TRYING TO FIX THE UNFIXABLE EXERCISE

A form of denial, lack of acceptance of situations as they are.

HUMBLE EXERCISE

Very important for progress, needing to think of others rather than just oneself, to be grateful, not unnecessarily self-important, yet recognizing and admitting one's own strengths, a balance comes to exist.

PRETENDING

Not being totally honest with oneself or others, it is often a learned form of lying and maybe unconsciously done, sometimes done to take care of another's feelings.